Pockets Full of Rocks

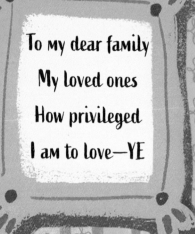

To my dear family
My loved ones
How privileged
I am to love—YE

To Anna, for being my
lighthouse during the
storms, and helping me
keep my own clouds
at bay—MH

Books for Kids From the
American Psychological Association

Story text copyright © 2021 by Yair Engelberg. Illustrations copyright © 2021 MacKenzie Haley. Note to Parents copyright © 2021 by Magination Press, an imprint of the American Psychological Association. All rights reserved. Except as permitted under the United States Copyright Act of 1976, no part of this publication may be reproduced or distributed in any form or by any means, or stored in a database or retrieval system, without the prior written permission of the publisher.

Magination Press is a registered trademark of the American Psychological Association.
Order books at maginationpress.org, or call 1-800-374-272..

Book design by Rachel Ross

Printed by Worzalla, Stevens Point, WI

Original English translation by Seree Zohar

Library of Congress Cataloging-in-Publication Data

Names: Engelberg, Yair, author. | Haley, MacKenzie, illustrator.

Title: Pockets full of rocks/by Yair Engelberg; illustrated by MacKenzie Haley.

Description: Washington, DC: Magination Press, [2021] | Summary: "A young daughter presents questions to her depressed father"—Provided by publisher.

Identifiers: LCCN 2020026806 (print) | LCCN 2020026807 (ebook) | ISBN 9781433831096 (hardcover) | ISBN 9781433834752 (ebook)

Subjects: CYAC: Depression, Mental—Fiction. | Fathers and daughters—Fiction.

Classification: LCC PZ7.1.E529 Pic 2021 (print) | LCC PZ7.1.E529 (ebook) | DDC [E]—dc23

LC record available at https://lccn.loc.gov/2020026806

LC ebook record available at https://lccn.loc.gov/2020026807

Manufactured in the United States of America

10 9 8 7 6 5 4 3 2 1

Pockets Full of Rocks

By Yair Engelberg

Illustrated by

MacKenzie Haley

Magination Press • Washington, DC • American Psychological Association

My daddy looks so sad. He stays in bed all day.
Mommy has to do everything!

One morning, I go to wake Daddy up.

I shake him gently, tug at his blanket,

and even tickle his toes.

"Daddy, get up!
What's wrong?
Why do you sleep so
much, and why don't
you smile anymore?"

Daddy rubs his eyes and slowly gets out of bed.

"Daddy, what's wrong?"
I ask again.

"I don't feel well,"
Daddy answers softly.

"Are you sick? Do you have a cut?
Should I bring you a bandage?"

"No, honey, that's not the problem."

"Oh! You didn't eat the cookies Mommy and I made for you. Does your tummy hurt?"

"No, Ella," answers Daddy. "My tummy is okay."

"Then what's wrong?"

Daddy picks me up, hugs me, and sits me on his lap.

"Daddy has something called depression,"
he says. "It makes me feel very sad and tired."

"Sad like me when you don't want
to play with me?" I ask softly.

"Depression is a bit like that, but stronger, and it doesn't go away as fast.

It's been hanging around inside me for a long time.

I still want to play with you, Ella—you haven't done anything wrong, and I love you as much as ever. Depression is just really annoying! It makes me want to stay in bed and not do things—even fun things, like playing with you."

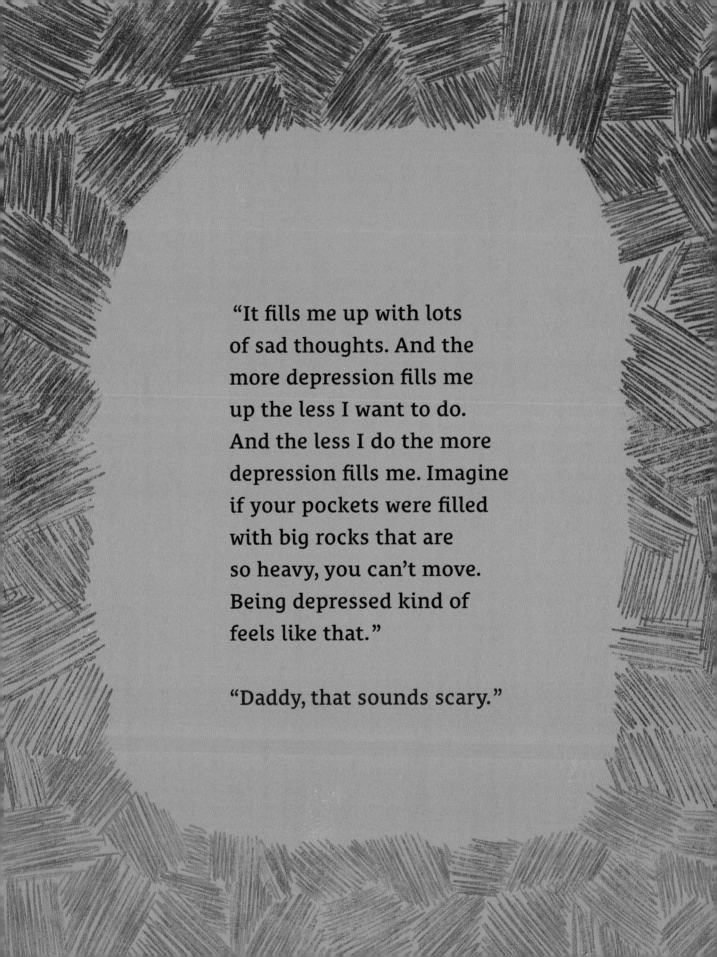

"It fills me up with lots
of sad thoughts. And the
more depression fills me
up the less I want to do.
And the less I do the more
depression fills me. Imagine
if your pockets were filled
with big rocks that are
so heavy, you can't move.
Being depressed kind of
feels like that."

"Daddy, that sounds scary."

"Oh, Ella, we can't let depression scare us," Daddy says, his voice calm.

"Lots of people get depressed, but they can learn to manage it and enjoy themselves and be with friends and family. It's not easy, but I'm trying."

"But how?"

"Talking like this helps. I talk to a therapist, too. I tell him about how depression makes me feel and what I think about. That helps me feel better."

"Riding my bike also helps a lot," Daddy adds. "Moving my body can help my sad feelings go away. Exercise gives me energy and keeps me moving.

And I also take medicine that helps my body and mind balance my feelings and thoughts. My therapist, my bike, and the medicine help me fight back against depression."

I'm a little worried.
"Will depression happen to me, too?"

"You can't catch depression like a cold. But if you ever feel like this, let me or Mommy know, and we can find ways to fight back against it, just like I'm doing."

"Can I help you?" I ask.

"I don't want you to worry—
it's not your job to fix me.
But hug me tight, and hug
me lots," Daddy says.

"That fills me up with strength and hope."

I hug Daddy as tight as I can, because I love him, and because I want to help squeeze depression out.

I really squash
that depression!
Daddy is all smiles.

Reader's Note

Depression is more than just sadness. Everyone feels sad or "blue" on occasion. There are many life experiences to grieve over, such as a major illness, a death in the family, a loss of a job, or a divorce. But, for most people, these feelings of grief and sadness tend to lessen with the passing of time. If a person's feelings of sadness last for two weeks or longer, and if they interfere with daily life activities, something more serious than "feeling blue" may be going on.

Talking to Children About Depression

It can be hard to know how to talk to children about depression. You want to reassure them that everything will be fine, but you also don't want to mislead them. The best course of action is to be straightforward while encouraging; recognize the struggles, and talk about what you're doing or can do to work on getting better. This book is meant to be a starting place for this conversation. It aims to present the topic in a simple, straightforward, and honest way, and to open the doors to a child's questions, concerns, and feelings.

Welcome All Feelings
Let children know that all feelings are okay. They shouldn't hesitate to express their emotions to you, even if they're negative ones. Explain that expressing feelings and talking openly can help resolve problems and make you both feel better.

Answer Questions Honestly
Use straightforward answers with enough information to reassure them, but without telling them things that might increase their worries or fears. For example, they don't need to know about the exact depths of the depression, or about possible self-destructive thoughts or behaviors. Avoid euphemisms and evasions. Children have vivid imaginations; if you try to avoid the questions, they may fill in worst case scenarios.

"Will I get depression too?"

Be honest: you can't catch depression like a cold. But if they're ever having persistent feelings of sadness and lethargy, they should talk to you or another trusted adult, and you will help them learn how to manage it.

"How can I make you better?"

Let them know how much their support and love means to you, and helps you through hard times, but be clear that it is not the child's job to fix the adult.

"Did I do something wrong?"

Be sure to emphasize that your depression is not the child's fault, and, again, it is not their job to fix it.

Reassure Them of Your Love
Depression might stop you from participating as much as you would like, but you will always love them. Nothing can change that. Acknowledge that sometimes you aren't able to show up, physically or emotionally, and allow them to feel upset about this. But always come back to the fact that you still love them as much as ever.

Don't Be Afraid to Ask for Help
If your depression won't let you adequately discuss this with your child, or meet your child's needs in other ways, get other trusted adults involved. Pay attention to your child's needs, both physical and mental. If you suspect that they may be at risk of depression themselves, treatment through therapy, medication, and exercise is just as helpful and effective for children as it is adults.

Coping With Depression

Depression is the most common mental health disorder. Fortunately, depression is treatable. A combination of therapy and antidepressant medication can help ensure recovery. You can discuss these methods, and your personal plan for treatment with your child, as much as is developmentally appropriate.

Therapy

There are many types of therapy that have been proven to be effective treatments for depression. A therapist can work with individuals with depression to:

- Pinpoint the life problems that contribute to their depression.

- Identify options for the future and set realistic goals that enable them to enhance their mental and emotional well-being.

- Identify negative or distorted thinking patterns. For example, depressed individuals may tend to overgeneralize—that is, to think of circumstances in terms of "always" or "never." They may also take events personally. A trained and competent therapist can help nurture a more positive outlook on life.

- Help people regain a sense of control and pleasure in life. Psychotherapy helps people see choices as well as gradually incorporate enjoyable, fulfilling activities back into their lives.

Family & Friends

The support and involvement of family and friends can play a crucial role in helping someone who is depressed. Individuals in the "support system" can help by encouraging a depressed loved one to stick with treatment and practice the coping techniques and problem-solving skills they are learning through psychotherapy.

Family or marital therapy may also be beneficial in bringing together all the individuals affected by depression and helping them learn effective ways to cope together. This type of psychotherapy can also provide a good opportunity for individuals who have never experienced depression themselves to learn more about it and identify constructive ways of supporting a loved one who is suffering from depression. It can also help allay the worries of the other members of the family—including children.

Medication

Medications can be very helpful for reducing the symptoms of depression in some people, particularly in cases of moderate to severe depression. Often a combination of psychotherapy and medications is the best course of treatment. However, given the potential side effects, any use of medication requires close monitoring by the physician who prescribes the drugs.

Some depressed individuals may prefer psychotherapy to the use of medications, especially if their depression is not severe. By conducting a thorough assessment, a licensed and trained mental health professional can help make recommendations about an effective course of treatment for an individual's depression.

Exercise

The most common treatments for depression are psychotherapy or medication, but psychologists have found that exercise is a third successful option. Both individual experiments and general findings repeatedly point to the power of exercise in the treatment of clinical depression and anxiety, including issues of self-esteem, weight loss and weight loss management, and addictions.

Start by talking with your physicians and therapists, as applicable, about what is possible and healthy for you. Start small; set manageable goals that don't seem overwhelming. Exercise doesn't have to mean an hour on a treadmill; it can mean going for a walk around the block, swimming, yoga, or even weight-lifting. It can be whatever makes sense for you. And it can be a way to reconnect with other people again—family and friends can get involved in activities with you, and help you set and keep to a routine.

Depression can seriously impair a person's ability to function in everyday situations. But the prospects for recovery for depressed individuals who seek professional care are very good. By working with a qualified and experienced therapist, people suffering from depression can help regain control of their lives.

Adapted from the APA website and from Why Are You So Sad? A Child's Book About Parental Depression *(Magination Press, 2002). For more information, visit apa.org/topics/depression*

Yair Engelberg

is a psychologist who is certified by the Schneider Cognitive Behavioral Therapy Training Program for Child and Youth Therapy. This is his picture book debut.
Visit psyedu.co.il/book

MacKenzie Haley

is an award-winning illustrator who also illustrated *Snitchy Witch*. She lives in Louisville, KY.
Visit mackenziehaley.com
f @MacKenzie Haley
🐦 @MacKenzieLea
📷 @mackenzie_haley

Magination Press

is the children's book imprint of the American Psychological Association. APA works to advance psychology as a science and profession and as a means of promoting health and human welfare. Magination Press books reach young readers and their parents and caregivers to make navigating life's challenges a little easier. It's the combined power of psychology and literature that makes a Magination Press book special.
Visit maginationpress.org
f 🐦 📷 📌 @MaginationPress